Josie Smith and Eileen

Josie Smith liked her new frock so much that her hands felt all tingly and her eyes felt shiny and happy and she couldn't say anything. She liked it when her mum pulled it over her head and it smelled all clean and new. And she liked it when she felt the full skirt and it was all smooth and shiny. But most of all she liked it when she went to the front door to go and show it to Eileen and saw that it was exactly the same pale blue as the pale blue sky above the black roofs and chimneys. Eileen came out to look and Josie's mum and Josie's gran came out and even Mrs Chadwick from the shop across the road came out. And Josie Smith whizzed round and round in her pale blue frock as blue as the sky and they all said, "Happy birthday, Josie Smith."

Other Young Lions Storybooks

Magdalen Nabb

Josie Smith and Eileen

Illustrated by Pirkko Vainio

Young Lions
An Imprint of HarperCollinsPublishers

First published in Great Britain by
William Collins Sons & Co. Ltd 1991
First published in Young Lions 1992

Young Lions is an imprint of
HarperCollins Children's Books,
a division of HarperCollins Publishers Ltd,
77–85 Fulham Palace Road,
Hammersmith, London W6 8JB

Printed and bound in Great Britain by
HarperCollins Manufacturing, Glasgow

Contents

Josie Smith and the Secret Party

Josie Smith's house was number one. It was the same as all the other houses in the street, and the street was the same as all the other streets on the side of the hill. On the top of the hill was a tower.

Josie Smith was sitting on her doorstep in the sunshine playing shop. Josie's doll was playing shop, too. Josie's mum had given her some peas and lentils to use for toffees, and a spoon to weigh them with and some paper bags from the drawer to put them in.

"Now then," said Josie Smith. "A quarter of toffees, was it? These are very nice, orange flavoured. Twenty pence, please."

Josie Smith gave her doll a bag of orange toffees and some bottle tops for change.

Eileen came out from next door with her squeaky doll's pram. "Are you playing?" Eileen said.

"You have to wait your turn," Josie Smith said. "It's a shop."

"It doesn't look like a shop," Eileen said. "You haven't got scales. I've got scales. And those are not real toffees, either, they're peas and lentils."

"If you don't want to buy anything," Josie Smith said, "you can't come in."

"All right," Eileen said. "I'll buy some peas."

"They're not peas," Josie Smith said. "They're peppermints." And she spooned some peppermints into a paper bag for Eileen.

"We can pretend to eat them," Eileen said.

"We can if you want," said Josie Smith. "But we haven't to put them in our ears, my mum said."

Eileen put the brake on her pram and sat down on the doorstep next to Josie

Smith. "We can play with my scales, if you want," she said.

"My shop's shut now," said Josie Smith.

"Mrs Chadwick's isn't shut," Eileen said.

The door of Mrs Chadwick's shop across the road opened and Gary Grimes came out and shouted: "Who's coming to Mr Scowcroft's allotment to dig for worms?"

"I'm not," Eileen said. "You get dirty."

"I am," Josie Smith said. "Because he gives you wages."

"You promised to play with me," Eileen said.

"I never," said Josie Smith. "And anyway, you're soft because you're scared of getting dirty."

Josie Smith and Gary Grimes started running up the street. "I'm telling over you!" shouted Eileen. "I'm telling my mum and she won't let you come to my party!"

Josie Smith stopped running and turned round.

"What party?" she said.

"My birthday party in two weeks and I'm having invitations with balloons on them and you can't come and Gary Grimes can't come, so there!"

"I don't care," said Josie Smith, but she said it with her eyes shut because she did care a bit. She looked down the street at Eileen and Eileen shouted, "*And* I'm getting a bride doll and you can't play with it."

"I don't care," shouted Josie Smith. "And it's my birthday before yours anyway."

"So what?" Eileen said. "You're not

having a party, my mum said."

Josie Smith shut her eyes as tight as she could and said, "I am having a party, just you wait and see."

"You are not," Eileen said. "And I bet you've got your eyes shut because you're telling a fib."

Josie Smith ran off up the street. Gary Grimes was waiting for her at Mr Scowcroft's allotment.

"Do you want us to dig for worms, Mr Scowcroft?" Gary Grimes said.

Mr Scowcroft sucked his pipe for a long time and then he said, "Aye."

Sometimes Josie Smith asked Mr Scowcroft why he always said Aye instead of Yes but he never told her. He only sucked on his pipe and looked at her.

Josie Smith did all the digging. She liked digging but Gary Grimes didn't, because it was hard work. Gary Grimes collected the worms in a tin to give to Mr Scowcroft's hens in the shed. Josie Smith didn't like collecting worms because they were cold and wriggly.

In the hen shed, where it was dark and

smelly, Josie Smith said, "D'you want to know a secret?"

"What is it?" Gary Grimes said.

"You have to promise not to tell," Josie Smith said.

"All right," Gary Grimes said. "Cross my heart and hope to die."

Josie Smith shut her eyes tight in the dark and said, "I'm having a party for my birthday the day after tomorrow."

"Can I come?" asked Gary Grimes.

"You can come," said Josie Smith and then she wagged her finger at Gary Grimes and said, "But you haven't to tell anybody because it's a secret party."

"I know a secret as well," Gary Grimes said. "Mr Scowcroft strangles his hens and eats them."

"He does not," Josie Smith said. "You don't eat real hens. You get chickens from a shop to eat."

"Well, anyway, ask Mr Scowcroft for our wages," Gary Grimes said. Josie Smith always had to ask for their wages because Gary Grimes was frightened of Mr Scowcroft.

Mr Scowcroft sucked on his pipe and looked at Josie Smith. Then he said, "You're a good little digger," and gave her a pure white egg.

When Josie Smith showed Gary Grimes the pure white egg, he said, "That's not wages, that's just a stupid egg."

"It is not," said Josie Smith. "It's special because it's pure white."

"Give it here and let's see," Gary Grimes said, and he grabbed the egg from Josie Smith and ran off down the street. Josie Smith ran after him as fast as her wellingtons would go, and her chest was going bam – bam – bam! because Gary

Grimes had stolen her pure white egg.

"It's mine!" shouted Josie Smith. "It's mine because I asked Mr Scowcroft! Because I'm a good digger!"

But Gary Grimes ran faster and faster down the street and in at his own front door. Bang!

Josie Smith stood near her front door. She was crying, and even though Gary Grimes had gone in she still shouted, "I'll get you for that, Gary Grimes! You're a robber and I'm telling!" Then she went in.

The next day, Josie Smith didn't play with Eileen because Eileen said she wasn't inviting her to her party. And she didn't play with Gary Grimes because he'd stolen her pure white egg. She played by herself and then, in the afternoon, she went to Mrs Chadwick's shop to buy cakes because her gran was coming for tea.

While they were having their tea, Josie Smith wanted to ask her mum if she could have a birthday party. She wanted to ask when her gran was there because sometimes when your mum says No, your gran says Yes.

But every time Josie Smith tried to ask, her mum said. "Hush! We're talking."

Grown-ups are always talking. They talk and talk about boring things and they get mad if you interrupt them. Josie Smith waited until the teapot was empty and her mum got up to fill it. Then she said, "Mum? Can I have a birthday party?"

"No," said Josie's mum.

"Why can't I?" said Josie Smith.

"Because we can't afford it," said Josie's mum.

"Gran?" said Josie Smith.

'You heard what your mum said," said Josie's gran. "Now be a good girl." Then she said, in a whisper, "Come here to me."

Josie Smith got down from her chair and went to her gran. Her gran had a magic handbag and sometimes a surprise came out of it for Josie Smith.

"Is there something in your magic handbag today?" asked Josie Smith.

"There might be," said Josie's gran. "You never know with magic handbags. Shut your eyes and feel inside."

Josie Smith shut her eyes and felt.

"Have you found anything?" said Josie's gran.

"A tube of toffees!" said Josie Smith.

"Well!" said Josie's gran, "I don't know how it is but you always find something. I never do. Put it in your pocket for after tea."

Josie Smith went back to her own chair. She liked the tube of toffees, but she was fed up. Her mum and her gran started talking again, but they didn't talk about Josie Smith having a birthday party. After a few minutes, Josie's mum said, "What's the matter with you? You're pulling a long face."

"I'm fed up," said Josie Smith. "Can I go in the front room and watch television?"

"No," said Josie's mum.

"Why can't I?" said Josie Smith.

"Because there's something in there you haven't to see," said Josie's mum.

"Is it a secret?" asked Josie Smith.

"That's right," said Josie's mum, "a secret. You go and play with Eileen for half an hour."

"I'm not friends with her," said Josie Smith.

"Well, make friends with her," said Josie's mum.

Josie Smith went to the front door and opened it. She looked up the street and down the street but Eileen wasn't there. Josie Smith got a bit of chalk out of her pocket and chalked big numbers on the pavement. Then she found a stone and started playing hopscotch by herself.

Eileen came out from next door and stood watching. She didn't say, "Are you playing?" She didn't say anything. Josie

Smith didn't say anything either, but when she was out she gave the stone to Eileen and Eileen played. When they'd finished playing, Eileen said, "If you want I'll give you an invitation to my party when I get them."

Josie Smith didn't say anything.

Then Eileen said, "Can I come to your party tomorrow?"

"All right," said Josie Smith. "Only, you haven't to tell anybody because it's a secret party."

"I won't tell anybody," Eileen said. "Am I still your best friend?"

"You are if you don't tell anybody," Josie Smith said. "Only Gary Grimes knows, and he can't come because he's a robber. He stole my pure white egg and I'm going to get him."

Down the street, the door of number eight opened and Gary Grimes came out. He came up the street pushing his model car along the windowsills. "Drrrrrrm! Drrrrrrm! Drrrrrrm!"

"I'm going to get you, Gary Grimes!" shouted Josie Smith. And when he came near she put her fist up and said, "You're a robber and you stole my pure white egg."

"A-aw! Gary Grimes is a robber," Eileen said.

"You shut up," Gary Grimes said. "Or I'll thump you."

Eileen got behind Josie Smith and hid because she was frightened of getting thumped. Gary Grimes went after her with his fist up but Josie Smith stopped him and pushed him down. Gary Grimes started crying.

"Wa-a-a-a-a-a-h!" roared Gary Grimes. "Wa-a-a-a-a-a-h! Wa-a-a-a-a-a-h!" And he started running away down the street shouting, "I'm going to play with Rawley Baxter! Wa-a-a-a-a-ah!"

"He won't play with you!" Josie Smith shouted after him. "Because you're too soft! You'll have to play with his little sister!"

When he'd gone into Rawley Baxter's house, Eileen said, "Gary Grimes is horrible. If he tries to thump me again I'm going to nip him and then I'm going to tell over him."

"You shouldn't nip," Josie Smith said.

"Well, anyway," Eileen said, "he's not coming to your secret party, is he?"

"No, he's not," Josie Smith said. "And if he goes and tells anybody I'll knock him down again."

Then some big clouds came and covered up all the blue sky in between the roofs and chimneys of Josie Smith's street. When they sat down on the doorstep it felt cold, and Eileen said, "Let's go into your front room and watch television."

"We can't," Josie Smith said. "My mum says I haven't to go into the front room because there's a secret."

"A secret like your party?" Eileen said. And then she said, "We can peep in through the window."

They put their noses right against the window but they couldn't see anything that looked like a secret.

"There's just your mum's sewing machine," Eileen said. "And some blue stuff that she's sewing. That's not a secret because she sews all the time."

Eileen's mum shouted from next door.

"Eileen? Eileen!"

"I've got to go in now," Eileen said.

Josie Smith wagged her finger at Eileen and said, "You haven't to tell *anybody* about my party, not even your mum because she'll tell my mum."

"I won't tell anybody," Eileen said.

Eileen didn't tell anybody, not even her mum.

But Gary Grimes told.

Gary Grimes told Rawley Baxter when he went to play at his house. "Josie Smith's having a party and I'm going to it," he said.

Then Rawley Baxter told.

When Gary Grimes had gone home, Rawley Baxter told his little sister. "Josie Smith's having a party and I'm going to it," he said.

The next day when Josie Smith woke up it was her birthday, and when she looked out of the window all the black roofs and chimneys were shining and the sky was pale blue. Then she got dressed and went downstairs.

"Happy birthday," said Josie's mum.

"Am I having a present?" said Josie Smith.

"At teatime," said Josie's mum. "When your gran comes."

"Can I go to my gran's now?" said Josie Smith. "And ask her something?"

"When you've finished your breakfast," said Josie's mum. "But don't stay there for your dinner because she's busy."

"I won't," said Josie Smith. She finished her breakfast and then she put her wellingtons on and ran outside. There was no sunshine in the street yet, but Josie Smith shut her eyes and sniffed and she could smell the sunshine coming, all fresh and hot somewhere in the pale blue sky behind the chimneys. She hopped all the way down the street to her gran's house, saying, "If you tread on a nick you'll marry a stick and a blackjack'll come to your wedding."

"Happy birthday," said Josie's gran.

"Am I having a present?" said Josie Smith.

"At teatime," said Josie's gran. "When I come to your house." Her gran's kitchen was warm and smelled of hot cake.

"Have you made jam tarts?" asked Josie Smith.

"I've made jam tarts and lemon tarts," said Josie's gran. "And you can have one now if you're hungry."

"And one for Eileen?" asked Josie Smith.

"And one for Eileen," said Josie's gran. "Here's a little bag for them."

"I'm saving them for after," said Josie Smith.

"After what?" said Josie's gran.

"It's a secret," said Josie Smith. "And

I'm saving the tube of toffees you gave me, as well, only I wish I had a bottle of pop." She looked at her gran very hard.

"Are you thirsty?" asked Josie's gran.

"No," said Josie Smith.

"Well, what do you want a bottle of pop for?" said Josie's gran.

"It's a secret," Josie Smith said. "I *wish* I had one."

"All right," said Josie's gran. "Seeing as it's your birthday," and she gave Josie Smith some money. "Go and get one from Mrs Chadwick's. And don't go pestering your mum, because she's going to have a very busy day with *her* little secret. You play out with Eileen."

Josie Smith went into Mrs Chadwick's shop and bought a bottle of pop.

"A red one," she said, "with two straws, one for me and one for Eileen."

Josie Smith hid the bottle of pop and the two straws and the bag of jam tarts and the tube of toffees in a corner of the back yard. Then she played with Eileen until dinner time.

After dinner, Eileen said, "What time

have I to come to your party?"

"At four o'clock," Josie Smith said. "And don't forget it's a secret and you haven't to tell."

"I haven't told," Eileen said.

But Gary Grimes had told. Gary Grimes had told Rawley Baxter.

And Rawley Baxter had told. Rawley Baxter had told his little sister.

And that day, Rawley Baxter's little sister ran round the corner and told all the children in Albert Street.

At four o'clock, Josie Smith was on the doorstep, ready. She still had her wellingtons on but she had a fancy striped frock on, too. And on the doorstep was some paper with flowers crayoned on it for a tablecloth and two saucers with jam tarts on them and a tube of toffees and a bottle of red pop with two straws.

Eileen came out from next door.

"Is it time for your party?" Eileen said.

"Yes," said Josie Smith. "You have to sit at that side and I have to sit on this side and our dolls can sit on our knees."

They sat on the doorstep and nibbled

their jam tarts. The sun came out from behind the chimneys in the pale blue sky and warmed their heads and knees and Eileen said, "Is that your best frock?"

"Yes," said Josie Smith.

"A-aw! Josie Smith!" Eileen said. "I bet your mum doesn't know you've got it on."

"She does," said Josie Smith, but she said it with her eyes shut because it was a lie.

"She does not," Eileen said. "Or else you'd have had your best sandals on as well and white socks like me."

They sucked some red pop through

their straws and then they heard a lot of noise.

"Somebody's coming," Eileen said. They stood up.

Gary Grimes was coming.

And Rawley Baxter was coming.

And Rawley Baxter's little sister was coming.

And behind Rawley Baxter's little sister came all the children from Albert Street. Some of them had parcels and some of them had plates of buns and one of them had a jelly shaped like a rabbit and Gary Grimes had Josie Smith's pure white egg.

"We've come to your party, Josie Smith," they said.

"I've brought your egg back," Gary Grimes said.

"Where is your party?" Rawley Baxter said. "Is it in your front room?"

Josie Smith didn't say anything. She didn't know what to say. She couldn't take Gary Grimes and Rawley Baxter and Rawley Baxter's little sister and all the children from Albert Street in the front room because her mum had said she hadn't to go in the front room and her mum didn't know about the party. And Gary Grimes and Rawley Baxter and Rawley Baxter's little sister and all the children from Albert Street wouldn't fit on the doorstep.

Josie Smith looked at all the children with their parcels and jelly and buns and then she said, "No, it's not in our front room because it's a secret party."

The children looked at Josie Smith and waited.

Then she said, "*And*, it's not in our front room because my mum's got a secret as well and that's in the front room."

The children looked at Josie Smith and waited.

Then she said, "So, it's a picnic!"

"A picnic?" said Gary Grimes.

"A picnic?" said Rawley Baxter.

"A picnic?" said all the children from Albert Street.

"A secret picnic," said Josie Smith. "Up on the hill. Everybody follow me!"

So Josie Smith and Eileen and Gary Grimes and Rawley Baxter and Rawley Baxter's little sister and all the children from Albert Street went up the street past Mr Scowcroft's allotment and past Josie Smith's school to the hill with a tower on top. When they got there, Josie Smith opened all the parcels and shared out all the food and had the best party in the world. There was cake and leapfrog and tig and toffees and crisps and buns and bananas and buttercups and bluebells and climbing up the hill and rolling down again and gob stoppers and daisy chains and wrestling matches and a jelly shaped like a rabbit. And there was a lot of fighting and shouting, and nobody said *Be quiet* and nobody said *Don't touch* and nobody said *You've got to eat your meat before your cake* because there were no grown-ups there to say it, and anyway, there was no meat. There was just sherbert and sticky buns with icing on, and biscuits and bubble gum and custard pies and liquorice and big red lollies.

And when everybody had made as much noise as they could and everybody had eaten too much and Gary Grimes had been sick, they all went home for their tea,

back down the hill and past Josie Smith's school and Mr Scowcroft's allotment and down the street to their own front doors. Gary Grimes went in and Rawley Baxter went in and Rawley Baxter's little sister went in and all the other children ran round the corner to Albert Street.

"I'm going in now," Josie Smith said.

"A-aw, Josie Smith!" Eileen said. "Look what you've done to your best frock!"

Josie Smith looked. It didn't look like a best frock any more. She'd spilled a lot of red pop down the front and there were grass stains down the back. One of the pockets had got ripped off when she was playing leapfrog and she'd torn the arm-holes rolling down the hill.

"A-aw, Josie Smith!" Eileen said. Eileen never got dirty.

Josie Smith started crying.

"You'll get smacked for that," Eileen said. Eileen never ripped her frock.

Josie Smith went in. She tried not to make a noise with her wellingtons and she kept her eyes shut so that nobody would see her in her dirty frock. Then she opened them and peeped in the kitchen. She saw her mum and her gran and the table set for tea and a big cake in the middle with candles on it.

"Wherever have you been?" said Josie's mum.

"Snnff!" said Josie Smith. She stared at the candles.

"Wherever did you find that frock?" said Josie's mum. "It's far too small for you. I was saving it to cut down for your doll!"

"You're not crying, are you?" asked Josie's gran.

"You haven't been fighting, have you?" asked Josie's mum.

"No," said Josie Smith. She stopped crying.

"Well, take that old frock off and get washed," said Josie's mum.

"And come and eat this big cake I've made you," said Josie's gran.

Grown-ups are really peculiar. Sometimes they shout and hit you when you haven't done anything at all, and sometimes when you've done hundreds of naughty things they don't notice.

Josie Smith wasn't hungry but she ate some of her cake because it had icing on and candles. After tea, her mum said, "Now you can come into the front room and see my secret."

Josie Smith and Josie's mum and Josie's gran all went in the front room together, and there on a chair was a brand new best frock, sky blue and shiny, for Josie Smith's birthday.

"Did you make it on your sewing machine?" asked Josie Smith.

"That's right," said Josie's mum. "I didn't want you to see it until it was ready. Come on, let's see how you look in it."

Josie Smith liked her new frock so much that her hands felt all tingly and her eyes felt shiny and happy and she couldn't say anything. She liked it when her mum pulled it over her head and it smelled all clean and new. And she liked it when she felt the full skirt and it was all smooth and shiny. But most of all she liked it when she went to the front door to go and show it to

Eileen and saw that it was exactly the same pale blue as the pale blue sky above the black roofs and chimneys. Eileen came out to look and Josie's mum and Josie's gran came out and even Mrs Chadwick from the shop across the road came out. And Josie Smith whizzed round and round in her pale blue frock as blue as the sky and they all said, "Happy birthday, Josie Smith."

Josie Smith at Eileen's

Josie Smith was having a boiled egg for tea. She liked having a boiled egg, because when it was ready and sitting in its eggcup, Josie's mum always drew a smiling face on it and a fringe with a felt-tipped pen. Josie Smith smiled at the smiling egg and called it Henrietta. Then she took the top off without spoiling the face and ate up the inside, dipping in with bread that her mum cut into soldiers.

After tea, Josie Smith sat at the kitchen table, crayoning. The curtains were drawn and the light was on because it was nearly bedtime. Josie Smith was good at crayoning, going round and round very carefully so that the colours came out strong and bright with no scribbly bits.

"Get ready for bed, now," said Josie's mum.

"Can I finish my picture first?" said Josie Smith.

"No," said Josie's mum. "You'll be hours."

"I won't be hours," said Josie Smith. "I'll only be five minutes. *Go* on."

"You can finish it tomorrow," said Josie's mum. "Put your crayons away."

Josie Smith put her crayons in their box in the right order so that they looked just like new.

"I haven't broken any," she said. "And

I haven't scribbled. Eileen scribbles."
Eileen was Josie Smith's best friend, but
she wasn't so good at crayoning.

"Hurry up," said Josie's mum. Then
she looked at Josie Smith's picture. It was
a picture of soldiers marching along in red
coats and black trousers, with people
cheering and a golden coach with a princess
peeping out. Josie Smith had copied some
of it from the book her mum had brought
her from the library and some of it she'd
made up herself.

"It's nice, is that," said Josie's mum.

Grown-ups are always saying things are
nice. They say it in a silly voice just so that
you'll go away and stop pestering. But this
time Josie's mum said it in a real grown-
up's voice, so Josie Smith knew that her
picture was good.

"Can I take my book to bed?" Josie
Smith asked.

"It's late," said Josie's mum.

"Just to keep under my pillow? Can I?"

"All right," said Josie's mum. "Now
hurry up, and don't forget to clean your
teeth."

When Josie Smith was in bed she kicked her feet under the bedclothes and said, "Mum?"

"Settle down," said Josie's mum.

"I am settling down," said Josie Smith. "Mum? When I grow up I'm going to be a soldier."

"I thought you wanted to be a ballet dancer," said Josie's mum. "And how many times do I have to tell you to fold your kilt up when you take if off instead of dropping it on the floor?"

"I forgot. Mum? I am being a ballet dancer as well as a soldier."

"All right. Now, settle down and stop kicking."

"Mum?" said Josie Smith. "I want to tell you something. You know Rawley Baxter? Well, he ran all the way down the back street being Batman when everybody's washing was out and he dirtied all the sheets and Eileen told over him and he says he's going to get her."

"Where's your hanky gone from this pocket?" said Josie's mum.

"I don't know. Mum?"

"I don't know why I bother giving you one when you lose it every day," said Josie's mum.

"*Mum*!"

"And it was one of those nice ones that your gran bought you for your birthday," said Josie's mum, "with a pink elephant on it. And look at the collar of this blouse, it's filthy!"

"*Mum*! Rawley Baxter says – "

"Never you mind what Rawley Baxter says, I've got something to tell you."

Josie's mum sat down on the bed with a funny look on her face that Josie Smith didn't understand, and she said: "Now then. You remember your Aunty Helen who lives in London?"

"She wears nail varnish," said Josie Smith.

"Well, she's going to have a baby," said Josie's mum.

"But she's got one already," said Josie Smith, "called Michael cousin."

"Cousin Michael," said Josie's mum, "not Michael cousin, and he's not a baby any more, he's three and he's going to have a little brother or sister."

"Can I have one, as well?" said Josie Smith.

"No," said Josie's mum.

"Why can't I?" said Josie Smith.

"Because you can't," said Josie's mum.

"Well, can I go to ballet dancing classes then?" said Josie Smith.

"Will you listen to what I'm telling you?" said Josie's mum. "I'm going to go down and stay with Aunty Helen for a couple of days to help her."

"Am I going as well?" asked Josie Smith.

"No," said Josie's mum, "because there isn't room."

"But who's going to look after me?" said Josie Smith. "If you go away?"

"That depends," said Josie's mum. "If you want you can stay at your gran's, but Eileen's mum says you can stay at Eileen's."

"At Eileen's!" shouted Josie Smith, bouncing up and down in bed. "At Eileen's! I'm going to sleep at Eileen's!"

"All right, all right. Settle down, now." Josie's mum switched the light off and started to go down.

"Mum!" shouted Josie Smith.

"What's the matter now?" said Josie's mum.

"Ginger's not here," said Josie Smith.

Ginger was Josie Smith's cat and he had his basket next to Josie Smith's bed.

"Ginger's outside, playing," said Josie's mum.

"But I want him to be in his basket," said Josie Smith, "so I can tell him about going to sleep at Eileen's. Why is he always going out to play in the dark?"

"Cats like playing out at night," said Josie's mum, "because they can see in the dark. I'll bring him up if he comes in. You get to sleep."

But Josie Smith didn't get to sleep for a long time because she was excited about going to sleep at Eileen's. Ginger didn't go to bed at all. He stayed outside all night, and the next day, when Josie Smith was reading her book about soldiers on the doorstep, he fell asleep, curled up tight in the corner in a little patch of sunshine.

Rawley Baxter came up the street being Batman. Rawley Baxter's sister was behind him.

Rawley Baxter said to Josie Smith, "Do you want to play? You can be Robin, if you want, instead of her. She always falls when we run fast."

"I'm not playing," Josie Smith said. "I'm reading."

"Books are rubbish," Rawley Baxter said. "What is it, anyway?"

"It's a book about soldiers," said Josie Smith. "I'm going to be a soldier when I grow up."

"You're not," Rawley Baxter said. "Only boys can be soldiers. Girls are too soft. You don't even want to play Batman."

"I am not soft," Josie Smith said. "I can bash you up, for a start and if you touch Eileen I *will* bash you up because she's my best friend."

"She's a tell-tale-tit," Rawley Baxter said, "because she told over me for dirtying everybody's washing." Then he said to his little sister, "Come on, you." And they ran away.

Josie Smith read her book out loud so that Ginger could listen. Ginger opened one eye and then closed it again.

Eileen came out from next door and sat down on the doorstep in between Josie Smith and Ginger. When Josie Smith stopped reading, Eileen said, "Is it the end?"

"No," Josie Smith said. "But I'm saving some of it for after, and when I grow up I'm going to be a soldier in a red coat like this one." And she showed Eileen the picture in her book.

"You said you were being a ballet dancer," Eileen said.

"I am being a ballet dancer," Josie Smith said. "And a soldier as well."

"I'm going to be a nurse," Eileen said. "And next Christmas I'm getting a nurse's uniform. You're coming to sleep at our house. My mum said. Is Ginger coming as well?"

"No," said Josie Smith. "Because cats don't like other people's houses. My mum said. Your mum's got to give him his dinner at our house and let him out at night to play."

"What does he want to play out at night for?" Eileen said.

"Because he can see in the dark," said Josie Smith.

Josie's mum opened the front door. She was carrying a big bag to take to London, and a little bag for Josie Smith to take to Eileen's.

"Come on," she said. "I'm ready." And they all went round to Eileen's house.

Before she went to catch the train, Josie's mum said, "Be a good girl. No fighting with Eileen. Eat what you're given. Mind your manners at the table. Don't forget to clean your teeth. Don't give Eileen's mum any trouble. Are you listening?"

"Yes," said Josie Smith. "But, Mum? I can be a soldier when I grow up, can't I?"

"I thought you wanted to be a ballet dancer," said Josie's mum. "Now mind what I say about behaving yourself."

"But *can* I?" said Josie Smith.

"Can you what?" said Josie's mum.

"Be a soldier," said Josie Smith.

"Of course you can, if you're brave and strong. Now, don't forget what I've said about fighting with Eileen, and remember to say Please and Thank you. I'll bring you a nice present when I come back." And Josie's mum went away.

Josie Smith and Eileen went upstairs to Eileen's room and bounced on the beds and giggled and hit each other with pillows and tipped Eileen's toys all over the floor and stared each other out and put their tongues out at each other and giggled and giggled so much that they felt hot and tired out. Then Eileen's mum shouted:

"Eileen! Josie! Come down for your tea!"

And they went down.

At the table they giggled and squeaked and spluttered and pulled faces, and Eileen's mum said, "Behave yourselves," and gave them each a boiled egg.

Josie Smith remembered to say Thank you. Then she remembered something else. She looked at the boiled egg that had no face on it, and she remembered Henrietta. Josie's mum always drew a smiling face on her egg. But Josie's mum had gone away, and now Josie Smith couldn't remember when she was coming back. The egg was pale and had no smile. Josie Smith was pale and she had no smile either. She had a big lump in her throat and she didn't want to eat the horrible egg.

"What's the matter?" said Eileen's mum. "Don't you like eggs?"

"Her mum draws on her egg," Eileen said. "I've seen her when I stay for tea."

"You don't draw on food," Eileen's mum said. "Now, get on with your tea. Take a piece of bread."

Josie Smith took a piece of bread. She remembered to say Thank you. Then she

remembered something else. Her mum always cut her bread into soldiers. But Josie's mum had gone away, and Josie Smith couldn't remember when she was coming back.

"Now what's the matter?" said Eileen's mum.

"Her mum always cuts her bread up into strips," Eileen said, "I've seen her when I stay for tea."

"You shouldn't mess with your food," Eileen's mum said. "You should eat it." Then she got up to make some more tea.

Josie Smith had a big cup of milky tea in front of her. She drank a little bit of it to make the lump in her throat go down, but it wouldn't go. Then she thought of something. While Eileen's mum wasn't looking she could cut her bread into soldiers herself. And there was some red jam. If she put red jam on them they'd be red soldiers. Josie Smith picked up her knife and reached out for the jam. All of a sudden something went splosh! Josie Smith's big cup of tea was spilt and the tea went everywhere. All over the tablecloth, all over the bread on her plate and all down her skirt and her legs and into her wellingtons.

"For goodness' sake!" shouted Eileen's mum and she pulled Josie Smith away from the table. The tea dripped down on to the floor.

"How on earth did you do that?" shouted Eileen's mum.

Josie Smith didn't say anything because she didn't know.

Eileen's mum tried to mop up the tea, but she had to move all the plates and take the tablecloth off and there were puddles everywhere and she was really mad.

Josie Smith stood very still with the tea going drip drip drip from her skirt on to the floor. Her legs were wet with the tea and the lump in her throat hurt and her face felt all hot because she was frightened.

"I want my mum," she said in a very small voice, but nobody heard her.

Eileen's mum was so mad that she made Josie Smith and Eileen go and put their pyjamas on and get ready for bed.

Eileen didn't say anything. She didn't

take any notice of Josie Smith. When they got into bed she just played with her doll. She undressed it and put a nightie on it. Josie Smith had brought her doll but it didn't have a nightie. She held it very tight under the bedclothes and waited for Eileen's mum to come up and switch the light off. But nobody came.

Josie Smith waited a long time and then she said to Eileen, "Is your mum coming?"

"No." Eileen said. "She has to see to the baby."

"Will nobody switch the light off?" said Josie Smith.

"No," Eileen said. "I sleep with the light on." And she turned over with her back to Josie Smith and played with her doll for a bit. Then she went to sleep.

Josie Smith didn't go to sleep. She was hungry and thirsty. How can you go to sleep when you're hungry and thirsty?

And the light was on. How can you go to sleep with the light on?

Then the baby started crying. You can't get to sleep when there's a baby crying.

Smith lay with her eyes wide open,

50

thinking. It's good fun going to stay at your friend's house, but then you want to go home. Josie Smith wanted to go home. She wanted her mum. She cried a little bit and then she stopped because what's the use of crying if nobody's listening?

Then the frightening noise started.

First of all there was a quiet but very angry voice. It didn't say any words, it just went, "Mmmmmmmmmmmmm!" Then there was a loud spitting noise that went, "Sssssshwt!"

Then a great big howling noise singing

a frightening song that went, "Eeeeow-ou-ooooh! Eeeeow-ou-ooooh!"

Josie Smith put her head under the bedclothes and her fingers in her ears and her chest was going bam-bam-bam! Under the bedclothes she cried as loud as she could even if nobody was listening, because it was better to listen to herself crying than hear that terrible noise. When she was too tired to cry any more she fell asleep.

The next day, when Josie Smith and Eileen were sitting on Eileen's doorstep cutting out, Josie Smith didn't feel so well. She liked cutting out but she didn't like it so much today, even though there was some gold paper. She had a big pain in her chest and it was hard to breathe.

Gary Grimes came out of his house. He came up to them and said to Eileen, "You'd better watch out, because Rawley Baxter's going to get you for telling over him."

"He is not," Josie Smith said. "Because if he tries to thump Eileen I'll bash him."

"Rawley Baxter can bash anybody," Gary Grimes said.

"Oh no he can not," Josie Smith said. "I'm stronger than he is and I'm going to be a soldier when I grow up, so he'd better watch out!"

"I'm going to tell him," Gary Grimes said, and he ran away.

Josie's gran came up the street with her shopping bag. She gave Josie Smith and Eileen a toffee each and then she said to Josie Smith, "I've just seen Eileen's mum in Mrs Chadwick's shop and she said you didn't eat anything at teatime yesterday. Why was that?"

"I don't know," said Josie Smith.

"Well," said Josie's gran. "Today you're going to come and have some dinner at my house. I'm making a potato pie. You'll like that, won't you?"

"Yes," said Josie Smith, and she went to her gran's for her dinner.

She ate a big plate of pie and her gran said, "Do you feel better now?"

"Yes," said Josie Smith. "But I've got a pain in my chest."

Josie's gran felt her forehead.

"Have I got a temperature?" asked

Josie Smith.

"No," said Josie's gran. "You're just fretting, that's all. Don't you like staying at Eileen's?"

"I like it a bit," said Josie Smith. "But I want to go home."

"Well, you'll be going home tomorrow when your mum comes back."

"But I don't want to sleep at Eileen's again tonight," said Josie Smith. "Because there's a noise."

"What sort of noise?" asked Josie's gran.

"A frightening noise," said Josie Smith, and she tried to copy the noise but it only sounded funny and her gran laughed.

"Don't tell me a big girl like you is frightened of a silly noise like that. You're not really frightened, are you?"

"No . . ." said Josie Smith, but she said it with her eyes shut because it was a lie.

"That's a brave girl," said Josie's gran. "Your mum will want to know you've been a brave girl while she's been away, won't she?"

"I *am* brave," said Josie Smith. "I'm

going to bash Rawley Baxter up if he tries to thump Eileen. He's bigger than me but I'm not frightened of him."

"It's not so brave to fight him if you're not frightened of him," said Josie's gran. "It's when you're frightened that you have to be brave."

Josie Smith thought for a bit and then she said, "Like when there's a noise?"

"That's right," said Josie's gran. "Did you tell Eileen's mum about the noise?"

"No," said Josie Smith. "Because she'll tell Eileen and Eileen'll tell Gary Grimes and Gary Grimes'll tell Rawley Baxter and he'll say I'm soft and I can't be a soldier when I grow up because I'm a girl."

"Well," said Josie's gran, "I won't tell anybody, and tomorrow your mum's coming home. You can be a brave little soldier for one more night, can't you?"

Josie Smith thought for a bit and then she said, "I think I'll just be a ballet dancer instead, and then I won't have to be brave, will I?"

"Oh, but you will," said Josie's gran. "Ballet dancers have to go on the stage and dance in front of hundreds of people and they have to jump high and not be frightened of falling. And then they have to travel to all sorts of different places and sleep in strange rooms where they're not used to things, just like you sleeping at Eileen's."

"And do they hear noises?" asked Josie Smith.

"All sorts of noises," said Josie's gran. "But they have to get to sleep just the same because they have to get up early to practise their dancing."

"Oh . . ." said Josie Smith.

Then her gran gave her a bun and she went back to Eileen's.

In the afternoon, Josie Smith and Eileen put their dolls to sleep in Eileen's squeaky doll's pram and pushed it to the end of the street. When they got to the corner, Rawley Baxter came running up to them and Gary Grimes was behind him. Rawley Baxter put his fist up near Eileen's face and said, "You told over me and I'm going to thump you!"

Eileen cried as loud as she could.

"Just you leave her alone," said Josie Smith. But Rawley Baxter pulled Eileen's cardigan and thumped her on the back and grabbed her doll out of the pram.

"Here, Grimesy!" he shouted. "Catch hold of her doll and we'll smash it up!"

Eileen roared and roared, but Josie Smith jumped on Rawley Baxter and knocked him down and hit him.

"Get off me!" shouted Rawley Baxter. "Get off me!"

"You leave Eileen alone," shouted Josie Smith, and when she let him get up he ran away. Then Josie Smith went over

to Gary Grimes and he gave Eileen's doll back to her and he said, "I never touched it! I never broke it!"

"Just you watch out, Gary Grimes, that's all!" shouted Josie Smith, and she took the doll and gave Gary Grimes a little push and he ran away.

Eileen was still crying. Josie Smith put her arm round her and said, "Here's your doll. You can stop crying now, nobody's going to get you."

But Eileen cried as loud as she could all the way home and her mum heard her and came out.

"What's going on?" said Eileen's mum. "What are you crying for?"

And Eileen roared and cried and said, "Josie Smith's been fighting!"

"*Fighting*?" said Eileen's mum.

"With Rawley Baxter and Gary Grimes," Eileen said. "And they threw my best doll about and now it's all scratched."

"I had to fight Rawley Baxter," Josie Smith said, "because – "

"Get in that house!" shouted Eileen's mum. And when they were in the kitchen she got hold of Josie Smith with hard fingers and shouted, "Just look at your clothes!"

Josie Smith looked. The pocket of her skirt was a bit ripped.

"And it's filthy!" shouted Eileen's mum.

Josie Smith didn't think it was filthy. There was only a bit of dirt on it, but Eileen's mum made her take it off and put one of Eileen's on.

Eileen said, "I never get dirty."

They had baked beans for tea. Josie Smith liked baked beans but she didn't like them as much today. She had to eat them very slowly because she was frightened of spilling them on Eileen's skirt and they went cold. Baked beans are not so good when they're cold.

"Your mum told me you'd eat anything you were given!" shouted Eileen's mum. "You've eaten baked beans before when you've been here for your tea. I don't know what to give you!"

Grown-ups are always shouting at you. Even when you don't knock anything over and you don't spill anything on your clothes and you're just sitting there and not doing anything at all, they *still* shout at you.

Eileen's mum said, "I'm going next door to your house to feed Ginger and put him out. You two can watch television for half an hour and then bed."

When they were in bed and Eileen was undressing her doll she said, "My best doll's scratched and it's all your fault." Then she went to sleep with the light on.

Josie Smith couldn't get to sleep with the light on.

Then she couldn't get to sleep because the baby started crying.

Then the noise started.

First the quiet, angry voice that went, "Mmmmmmmmmmmm!" Then the loud, spitting noise that went, "Ssssshwt!" Then the great big howling noise singing a frightening song that went, "Eeeeow-ou-ooooh!"

Josie Smith got under the bedclothes and shut her eyes tight and stuck her fingers in her ears and heard her chest

going bam-bam-bam! Then the noise stopped and she went to sleep.

The next day, Josie Smith and Eileen played at going shopping. They put their dolls in Eileen's squeaky doll's pram and set off down the street. Eileen was carrying one of her mum's handbags over her arm and she was pushing the doll's pram with both hands. She only let Josie Smith hold on to the pram handle with one hand because it was her pram. Josie Smith felt tired and she still had a big pain in her chest because she was fretting. When they got to the corner and turned round, Josie Smith said, "It's my turn to carry the handbag."

"You can't carry it," Eileen said. "It's my mum's and she said I haven't to let you touch it because you dirty things."

"She never," Josie Smith said.

"She did," Eileen said. "Only I can play with it."

"I'm not playing, then," said Josie Smith.

"You have to play with me," Eileen said. "Or else I'll tell over you and my mum'll smack you."

"You're always telling over people," Josie Smith said. "You told over Rawley Baxter for dirtying everybody's washing and then you told over me for fighting him. I never tell over people."

"You can't tell over anybody," Eileen said, "because you've got no mum to tell!"

"I have!" shouted Josie Smith.

"You have not," Eileen said. "She's gone away and she's never coming back and you're not staying at our house any more because I'm not friends with you so you'll have to sleep outside on the doorstep!"

When they got back to their own end of the street, Eileen went in her house and shut the door.

Josie Smith went and sat on her own doorstep. She looked up the street and down the street but her mum wasn't coming. Josie Smith waited and waited and waited, but her mum didn't come. The pain in her chest was so big with fretting that she felt as if she would burst. She tried not to start crying but the pain in her chest made some tears squeeze out of her eyes. She rubbed them away hard but some more came. She didn't want Eileen to come out and see her crying so she put her head down on her knees.

"I want my mum," she whispered to her wellingtons, and then she started crying hard. She cried hard for a long time and then she felt somebody's hand on her head and a voice said, "Josie."

And when she looked up, her mum was there!

"You're not crying, are you?" asked Josie's mum.

"No," said Josie Smith with her eyes shut tight.

"Come on in," said Josie's mum, "and we'll have a nice cup of tea."

Then Josie's gran came and brought some cakes and they all had some tea.

"I didn't like it so much at Eileen's," Josie Smith said.

"Why was that?" said Josie's mum.

"Because there was a noise," said Josie Smith. "It went, 'Mmmmmmmmmmmmm!' and then it went, 'Ssssssht!' and then it went, 'Eeeeow-ou-ooooh!'"

Josie's mum laughed and then she said, "I know who made that noise and you know him, too. It's somebody who plays out at night and sits on the roof and sings, only he's not a very good singer."

"Who is it?" said Josie Smith.

"It's Ginger!" said Josie's mum.

"I didn't know it was Ginger," said Josie Smith, "or I wouldn't have been frightened."

"Well, that just goes to show," said

Josie's mum, "that you should always do your best to be brave, because sometimes the things you get frightened of are really not frightening at all. Isn't that right, Ginger?"

"Eeeow," said Ginger, and he looked at Josie Smith and made her laugh.

"And now," said Josie's mum, "I've got a present for you." And she took a parcel out of her bag and inside the parcel was a see-through box and inside the box was a beautiful soldier in a bright red coat. "A brave little soldier," said Josie's mum. "Just like you."

Josie Smith and the Wedding

Josie Smith was eating her dinner, but she didn't like it. The sun was shining and she wanted to play out with Eileen from next door, but she had to finish her dinner first.

"I don't like my meat," said Josie Smith.

"Sit up straight," said Josie's mum, "and finish your dinner."

When you don't like your dinner, the things on your plate get bigger and bigger instead of getting smaller, but Josie Smith had a special trick that she did when she didn't like her dinner. She copied everything that her mum did. When her mum ate a little bit of meat Josie Smith ate a little bit of meat, and when her mum got a little bit of potato and some peas on her fork, Josie Smith got a little bit of potato and some peas on *her* fork. When her mum drank a sip of water, Josie Smith drank a sip of water, and when her mum looked out of the kitchen window and made creases in her forehead, thinking, Josie Smith looked out of the kitchen window and made creases in *her* forehead, thinking.

"What's the matter?" said Josie's mum. "You've got a very serious face," and she ate some potato and gravy.

"I'm eating my dinner," said Josie Smith, and she ate some potato and gravy. Then she said, "Mum? I've finished. Can I look at Emmeth's wedding dress before I go out?"

"She's not called Emmeth," said Josie's mum. "She's called Emma. Wash your hands first and I'll show it to you. But remember what I've said to you about going in the front room by yourself when I'm making wedding clothes. One spot and they're ruined!"

Josie Smith washed her hands. The front room where her mum did her sewing was full of pieces of white and pink material and bits of lace and tissue paper.

"Now then," said Josie's mum, and she lifted up the wedding dress on its hanger and uncovered it. Josie Smith held her breath and looked. It made a soft rustling noise and the skirt was shiny and white as icing and the bodice was frothy and white like blossom.

"Do you like it?" said Josie's mum.

"Yes," whispered Josie Smith, and her mum covered the dress up again.

"Will I get married when I'm big?" asked Josie Smith.

"Of course you will," said Josie's mum.

"And I'll make you a dress like this one. Who are you going to marry? Gary Grimes?"

"No," said Josie Smith, "because he's soft. I'm going to marry Rawley Baxter."

"I see. And do you know who Emma's going to marry?" asked Josie's mum.

"No," said Josie Smith.

"She's going to marry Eileen's Uncle Simon," said Josie's mum.

"But you can't get married to an uncle," said Josie Smith.

"He's not Emma's uncle," said Josie's mum. "He's only Eileen's uncle."

"And will she have to kiss him?" said Josie Smith.

"Of course she will," said Josie's mum.

"Well, I'm not getting married then," said Josie Smith. "Because I'm not kissing Rawley Baxter. He keeps dirty things in his pockets."

"Does he?" said Josie's mum.

"Yes," said Josie Smith. "Bits of dirty string and stones, and a dead beetle in a matchbox, and I don't like the smell. Can I go and play out?"

When Josie Smith went and opened the front door to go out, she saw Mrs Chadwick from the shop across the road coming with Emma. Mrs Chadwick was Emma's mum and Emma was coming to try her wedding dress on.

"Hello, Josie," Mrs Chadwick said. "Is your mum in?"

"Yes," said Josie Smith, and then she shouted, "Mum! Mrs Chadwick's come and Emmeth!"

"Not Emmeth," Mrs Chadwick said. "*Emma*."

"Emmeth," Josie Smith said, shutting her eyes, because if she really wanted to she could say Emma, but she liked saying Emmeth.

When Mrs Chadwick and Emma had gone in and shut the door, Josie Smith went next door and called for Eileen. Eileen opened the door. She was holding a brand new bride doll. It had a long white frock on that was nearly as nice as Emma's wedding dress, and a veil and blonde curly hair like Eileen's.

"Are you playing?" Josie Smith said.

"I am, but we have to play in," Eileen said. "Because I'm playing with my bride doll and if I play out I'll dirty her."

"It's not your birthday," Josie Smith said. "You said you were getting a bride doll for your birthday."

"My mum said I could have it now," Eileen said, "for a special reason. I'm having something else for my birthday and I've got a secret as well and I haven't to tell it to you, my mum said."

"I don't care," said Josie Smith, but she said it with her eyes shut because it was a lie. When she opened her eyes again she looked at Eileen's bride doll, all white and pink and new with a frilly dress like Emma's and blonde curly hair like Eileen's, and she felt a lump coming in her throat to make her cry because she hadn't got one too. But she didn't cry. She said, "I'm going to call for Gary Grimes."

"I don't care," Eileen said, and she smiled a pretend smile and held her bride doll very tightly and then she went in and shut the door.

Josie Smith ran away, but she didn't

call for Gary Grimes. She ran up the street to the spare ground near Mr Scowcroft's allotment and picked a lot of flowers. She picked dandelions and buttercups and daisies, and some white flowers and purple flowers that she didn't know the names for, and took them all back to her doorstep. Then she sat down and got some silver paper and white paper and a crayon out of her pocket. She made the flowers into bouquets with silver paper round the stems, and she crayoned a notice saying FLOWERS FOR SALE. Then she waited for some customers to come. Eileen came out on her doorstep, holding her bride doll, but she didn't come into Josie Smith's flower shop.

Gary Grimes came. He came up the street from his house, running a dirty little car along the windowsills and going, "Vrrrum! Vrrrum! Vrrrum!" When he got to Josie Smith's doorstep he stopped.

"What are you doing?" he said.

"It's a flower shop," Josie Smith said. "And you can only come in if you buy some flowers."

"I haven't got any money," Gary Grimes said.

"You don't have to have real money," Josie Smith said. "It can be pretend."

"I want some white ones, then," Gary Grimes said.

"You can't have those," Josie Smith said. "Because they're for a wedding. You can only have dandelions."

"I don't want dandelions," Gary Grimes said. "If you don't give me some white ones I'll thump you."

"Oh no you won't," said Josie Smith.

"Because if you try I'll knock you down. You can have some dandelions and you have to pay me something for them."

Gary Grimes gave Josie Smith a caramel. It was a bit squashed, but it still had the paper on it and it wasn't dirty. Josie Smith gave him a bunch of dandelions and he went away, pushing his dirty little car along the windowsills and going, "Vrrrum! Vrrrum! Vrrrum!"

Eileen stood on her doorstep, holding her bride doll tightly and watching, but she didn't come into Josie Smith's flower shop.

Rawley Baxter came. He came running up the street with his anorak tied round his neck, being Batman, and his little sister was running behind him. When they got to Josie Smith's doorstep, they stopped.

"What are you doing?" Rawley Baxter said.

"It's a flower shop," Josie Smith said. "And you can only come in if you buy something."

"I haven't got any money," Rawley Baxter said.

"You don't have to have real money,"

Josie Smith said. "You can give me something else."

"I'll have some white flowers, then," Rawley Baxter said. "I can give them to my mum."

"You can't have those," Josie Smith said. "Because they're for a wedding. You can only have dandelions."

"Dandelions are rubbish," Rawley Baxter said. "Anybody can pick dandelions."

"These are special," Josie Smith said. "They're specially big and they're perfect *and* they've got silver paper round them."

"All right," Rawley Baxter said, and he took a bunch of dandelions and then he said, "Here. You can have this dot-to-dot picture out of my comic." And he took a folded up bit of paper out of his pocket.

"I don't want it if it's dirty," Josie Smith said. "And I don't want it if you've scribbled on it."

"I haven't scribbled on it," Rawley Baxter said. He gave the dot-to-dot picture to Josie Smith. Then he said to his little sister, "Come on."

But Rawley Baxter's little sister wouldn't go.

"What's the matter with you?" Rawley Baxter said. "Come on!"

But Rawley Baxter's little sister wouldn't go. She didn't say anything but she started crying.

"What's the matter?" said Rawley Baxter.

"What's the matter?" said Josie Smith.

Rawley Baxter's little sister kept on crying and she wouldn't go.

"I know what," said Josie Smith. "Perhaps she wants some flowers. Do you want some flowers?"

Rawley Baxter's little sister stopped crying and waited. Josie Smith gave her a little bunch of daisies with silver paper round the stems.

"You have to pay for them," Rawley Baxter said.

Rawley Baxter's little sister held her bunch of daisies with one hand and with the other she felt in her pocket for a long time. Then she pulled out a pink brooch and gave it to Josie Smith.

"Are you sure you don't want it?" said Josie Smith.

"It's all right," Rawley Baxter said. "It's not hers. She found it down at the swings. Come on."

Rawley Baxter ran off down the street being Batman and his little sister ran behind him.

Eileen stood on her doorstep, holding her bride doll tightly and watching, but she didn't come into Josie Smith's flower shop.

Josie Smith tidied her flowers a bit and hummed a little tune. Then she fastened

the pink brooch on her cardigan, unwrapped the caramel and put it in her mouth, and settled down to do the dot-to-dot picture with a crayon. She had almost finished doing it when somebody came into her shop. It was Eileen with her new bride doll.

"Can I buy some flowers?" Eileen said.

"It depends," Josie Smith said.

"But can I?" Eileen said. "I'll let you hold my bride doll after."

"All right, then," said Josie Smith. "You can have my best white ones because they're for a wedding and your bride doll can hold them."

"She can walk up and down with them, as well," Eileen said. "She's a walkie doll."

Josie Smith put the bouquet of white flowers wrapped in silver paper into the bride doll's sharp fingers.

"Have I got to pay for them?" Eileen said.

"No," Josie Smith said, "because you're my best friend, only you haven't to be horrible."

Then she jumped up and said, "I know!

Let's dress up as brides and pick some more flowers for wreaths and bouquets."

So they both ran into their houses and when they came out again they had their mums' old petticoats on over their frocks.

"Yours is ripped at the back," Eileen said. "The lace is hanging off."

"It doesn't matter," Josie Smith said. "You can't see it because it's at the back."

They left Eileen's bride doll on Josie Smith's doorstep, and ran up the street to the spare ground to pick some more flowers. Josie Smith was good at picking flowers. She chose the biggest ones and picked them very carefully. Eileen just picked anything and she ripped them up so that the roots and earth came with them.

"Mine aren't as good as yours," Eileen said.

"You shouldn't rip them up," Josie Smith said, and she cleaned the roots and earth off Eileen's flowers very carefully with her nails and fingers. She threw some of them away because they were no good. Then they crouched down and picked some more.

"There aren't any white ones left," Eileen said. "You have to have white ones for a wedding."

Josie Smith stood up and looked around. There were no white flowers left on the spare ground, but next to the spare ground, on the opposite side to Mr Scowcroft's allotment, there was a fence and the fence had white flowers poking through it.

"We can pick some of those," whispered Josie Smith.

"A-aw! Josie Smith!" Eileen said. "Those are Mrs Steeple's flowers. They're in her garden. You haven't to go in people's gardens, your mum said, and last time you went in somebody's garden you got smacked!"

"I'm not going in," said Josie Smith. "We can pick the flowers that are poking through the fence."

"It's stealing," Eileen said.

"Oh no it's not," Josie Smith said. "Because if they poke through the fence they're on the spare ground and anybody can pick them."

So they picked the flowers that were

poking through the fence. Then they made wreaths and put them on their heads.

"We need some more for our bouquets," Josie Smith said, and she was just reaching in to make another white flower come poking through the fence when a frightening voice shouted:

"Who's that picking my flowers? Josie Smith!"

Josie Smith and Eileen dropped their flowers and started running away as fast as they could. They ran down the back behind their houses and hid behind some washing that was hanging on a line. They were out of breath and frightened and Josie Smith's chest was going bam-bam-bam! They peeped out from behind a wet sheet and saw Mrs Steeple go past the corner. She was marching fast with her elbows out and a bad-tempered face.

"She's going to your house," Eileen said. "She'll tell your mum over you."

"Well," Josie Smith said, "she'll tell over you, as well."

"She will not," Eileen said, "because it was you who stole her flowers, I only held them."

"You're a liar," Josie Smith said, and then she started crying because she was frightened of Mrs Steeple.

"Anyway, she never saw me," Eileen said. "And you've had it now, because Mrs Steeple's a witch and she'll get you! She's got black hair and purple lipstick and she gets people when it's dark."

Then Josie's mum shouted, "Josie? Josie!"

They ran up the back and round the corner to their front doors. When they got there Josie's mum had gone in. Eileen picked her bride doll up and said, "I'm not playing with you tomorrow because you've been stealing, and anyway, tomorrow I'm being a bridesmaid at my uncle Simon's wedding and it's a secret. Your mum's making my frock and you can't come."

"I can if I want," said Josie Smith.

"Oh no you cannot," Eileen said. "Because it's my uncle and, anyway, you can't be a bridesmaid because you're ugly and you haven't got curly hair." And Eileen went in.

Josie Smith's front door opened and her mum came out in a bad temper and shouted, "So there you are! What have I told you about going in people's gardens?"

"I haven't to," said Josie Smith, and she was still crying.

"I'll give you something to cry about in a minute!" shouted Josie's mum.

"I never went in her garden," said Josie Smith. "I never!"

"Don't you tell me lies," shouted Josie's mum. "I'll give you such a tanning, young lady! And just when I'm so busy with this wedding! I'll be up all night finishing Eileen's frock as it is and you have to choose now to go and get yourself into trouble. Get in that house and get washed!"

Josie Smith went in and she was still crying.

She stopped crying to have her tea but she cried again under the bedclothes when she went to bed. She cried because she was frightened of Mrs Steeple with her black hair and purple lipstick. She might really be a witch. Then she cried because she hadn't got a fancy new bride doll like Eileen's. She only had a scratched old baby doll with a horrible frock. Then she cried because she felt sorry for her scratched old baby doll for not loving it and wanting a bride doll instead. She held her doll tight under the bedclothes and loved it and sniffed its eyelashes. Then she cried because she was ugly and didn't have curly hair and couldn't be a bridesmaid like Eileen. When she'd finished crying she went to sleep.

The next day was Saturday, and Josie

Smith had nobody to play with all morning. She sat on the doorstep with her doll in the sunshine, but nobody came out to play. Gary Grimes didn't come because he'd gone shopping with his mum. Rawley Baxter didn't come and Rawley Baxter's little sister didn't come because they'd gone to the park with their dad. Eileen didn't come because she was having her hair done specially to be a bridesmaid in the afternoon. When she came back from the hairdresser's with her mum, they went into Josie Smith's house for Eileen to try her bridesmaid's frock on. Josie Smith stayed on the doorstep. When they came out, Eileen's mum was carrying a shiny pink frock over her arm and Eileen said:

"I'm having a wreath as well and a posy in a basket. You're not coming to the wedding."

Josie Smith went in for her dinner.

After dinner, Josie's mum said, "I'm worn out. I'm going to have a little sleep. Now, don't you go away from that doorstep."

Josie Smith went out and sat on the doorstep. There was still nobody to play with. Then Eileen came out. She had the long shiny pink frock on and a wreath of pink rosebuds in her curly golden hair and frilly white gloves and white socks and sandals, and she was carrying a posy in a basket. She didn't say anything to Josie Smith. She went off down the street with her mum to Emma's wedding.

Josie Smith sat on her doorstep and squeezed her doll tightly against her chest. Then Mrs Chadwick came out. She was all dressed up in new yellow clothes and she had a lot of lipstick on. When she saw Josie Smith, she came across the street and said, "You look fed up. What's the matter? Is it because Eileen's being a bridesmaid and you're not?"

"No," said Josie Smith, but she said it with her eyes shut because it was a lie.

"Never you mind," Mrs Chadwick said. "You can come down to the church with your mum and see them all come out. Wouldn't you like to see Emma come out of church in her white frock?"

"Yes," said Josie Smith.

"Here," said Mrs Chadwick, and she

gave Josie Smith a packet of confetti from her handbag. "That's for you to throw. Now, mind you come with your mum because it's across the main road. Don't you set off by yourself. Promise?"

"Yes," said Josie Smith and she held her doll and the packet of confetti tightly against her chest and said, "Thank you, Mrs Chadwick." Then she ran to tell her mum.

Josie's mum was in the front room, lying on the settee fast asleep. All around her on the table and the chairs and the carpet there were bits of cloth and thread.

"Mum," whispered Josie Smith. But her mum didn't wake up.

"Mum," said Josie Smith a bit louder. But her mum didn't wake up. Her eyes were shut tight but she said in a sleepy voice, "Go and get something to play with. I've been up half the night and I want five minutes peace."

Josie Smith sat down on a chair with scraps of material and thread on it and held her doll and her bag of confetti tightly against her chest, waiting.

When grown-ups say five minutes you never know how long it will be. When you have to go to bed in five minutes it's very short but when they want five minutes' peace it goes on for a long time.

Josie Smith waited a long time and then she whispered, "Mum."

Josie's mum was snoring now.

"Mum," said Josie Smith a bit louder. "Have five minutes gone past yet?"

Josie's mum opened her eyes just a bit and then shut them again. She said in a sleepy voice, "Why don't you go out and watch Emma setting off?"

Josie Smith heard a car door banging and she jumped up and ran to the window. There was a big black car with white ribbons on the front of it outside Mrs Chadwick's shop. Josie Smith ran as fast as she could to the front door, but when she opened it the car was going away down the street. Josie Smith sat down on the doorstep with her doll and her packet of confetti and waited.

Sometimes five minutes is a *very* long time.

Then the front door opened and Josie's mum came out to shake a rug.

Josie Smith jumped up. "Mum?" she said. "Mrs Chadwick said we can go and watch Emmeth coming out of church in her white frock and I've got some confetti to throw!"

"You can't go," said Josie's mum. "It's across the main road." And she shook the rug harder because the bits of thread wouldn't come off.

"But you can take me," Josie Smith said. "Mrs Chadwick said you can take me."

"Don't start pestering," said Josie's mum. "I've enough to do as it is. The whole house is upside down."

"But *Mum*!" said Josie Smith, and she started to cry.

"Whatever's the matter with you?" said Josie's mum. "And stand out of the way, you're getting dust all over you."

"I want to see Emmeth in her white frock," said Josie Smith, and two big tears rolled down her cheeks.

"Well, you will see her," said Josie's

mum. "She'll be coming back in the car and when she gets out you can throw your confetti. Why don't you make her a wedding card while you're waiting?"

"With silver paper on it?" asked Josie Smith.

"If you like," said Josie's mum. "I've saved you a piece somewhere, I think it's on the shelf in the kitchen."

"And can I have a clean sheet of writing paper and make it really nice?" said Josie Smith.

"All right," said Josie's mum. "Just this once."

Josie Smith ran in behind her mum. When she came out, she was dressed up in her mum's long white petticoat and her wellingtons. She sat down on the step next to her doll with some clean paper and scissors and paste and silver paper and her crayons, and started to make a card for Emma.

On the front of it she stuck two silver paper bells with *WEDDING BELLS* written underneath in blue crayon. Inside she crayoned a bouquet of flowers and wrote

LOVE FROM JOSIE. Then she stood up and held the card and her packet of confetti, waiting. She waited a long time, and then the big black car with white ribbons on the front came slowly up the street and stopped outside Mrs Chadwick's shop.

Emma got out in her beautiful white dress. Josie Smith held her breath and looked at her and then she shouted, "Emmeth! Emmeth! I've made a card for your wedding!" And she went up to Emma and held it out.

"Oh," said Emma, bending down. "Isn't that nice! Is your mum in, Josie?"

"Yes," said Josie Smith, "but we couldn't come to the church because the house was upside down and we had to wait five minutes."

"Well," said Emma, "I want you to give her this because she worked so hard and did such a wonderful job on the dresses."

And Emma held out her big bouquet of perfumed white flowers.

"Carry it carefully," Emma said.

"Yes," whispered Josie Smith, and her arms were filled with the big white flowers that touched her face, all soft and cool, and she could hardly breathe with the perfume.

"Mind you don't drop it," Emma said.

Josie Smith set off back to her doorstep, holding the bouquet very carefully and taking small steps so that she wouldn't fall. Over the tops of the big flowers she saw her mum come to the door.

"Look!" said Josie Smith. "Mum! Look!"

"Well, what a nice thought," said Josie's mum. "I don't know where we'll find a vase big enough." And then she said, "You look like a real bride, now, with your long skirt and the flowers."

"Mum," said Josie Smith. "Can I carry it up and down? Just for a minute? Can I?"

"Go on, then," said Josie's mum. "But give me your packet of confetti, you can't manage both. Now, let's see how nicely you can walk."

Josie Smith set off down the street. She had to be very careful not to tread with her wellingtons on the ripped bit of petticoat that was trailing behind her, but she got to the bottom of the street without tripping up. Then she saw Eileen coming back in her pink bridesmaid's frock, holding her mum's hand.

"Well," Eileen's mum said. "What's this? Another wedding?"

"Yes," Josie Smith said. "And I'm the bride."

And Eileen said, "I can be your bridesmaid, can't I, Josie Smith?"

"All right," said Josie Smith. "You have to walk behind me."

And they set off back up the street. Josie's mum and Eileen's mum and Mrs Chadwick all sang, "Here comes the bride." The people in the other houses heard them and came out to watch Josie Smith's wedding. Gary Grimes came out and Rawley Baxter came out and Rawley Baxter's little sister came out. And when they got back to Josie Smith's house, Josie's mum threw the confetti. Josie Smith stopped and put the cool white flowers near her face and sniffed, and the coloured flakes of confetti twirled round and round her. And when she saw Mrs Chadwick

pointing her camera to take a photograph she tried to hold her big bouquet with one arm so that she could hold Eileen's hand.

"Smile," said Mrs Chadwick, and Josie Smith and Eileen held hands and smiled. Because even if Eileen was horrible sometimes, she was still Josie Smith's best friend.